ISBN: 978-0-359-56368-5

1

Contents

For GG, G-Daddy, Gaga, Paw Paw, Granny, and Grandad

Foreword

Honestly, this story is going to be terrible.

This entire story was a spark inside my head. I was writing something else, which I hopefully will revisit, but I got bored. So, I started another story. Then I got bored of that, too. So, I started this.

I was in a little hotel down near Mercedes-Benz stadium. We had been visiting supercross when this little seed planted inside my head. The tree became horribly crooked and weird. It was grotesque and scary.

Before I had been reading *The Shining* (I still am reading it. It's like six hundred pages!). Stephen King somehow inspired me to get this made. If he hadn't, this piece I have published would disappear. Vamoose.

His words seem to jump off the page and begin to speak. And I began the rigorous process of writing my short story, *The Chime* (Fun fact: my friends jokingly told me to name this *The Chiming*) (Another thing, if somethings in italics it is a thought)

The FIRST Day

The clock began its tick-tocking song at the hour of 5 AM. It had before been stopped by a pencil jammed in its gears to prevent its horrific music that faintly echoed through the halls, but the pencil was snapped and splintered (It didn't affect its powerful muffling powers, though).

It was a sight to see, that grandfather clock with its silver pendulum (It had a fine coat of rust) and maple wood lining. Its unique design would catch the eye of any person, even the ones that despised anything to do with antiques. (This clock had been crafted in the late 19th century in France. His Great Great Grandfather had brought it to America in his mid-twenties)

Alfred Lee had pride in this grandfather clock that he owned. His mind would screech *WAKE UP!* at 4:55 (Or at least around 4:55) to tell him to get out of bed and turn the clock operational. It may have been annoying to constantly do this, but it was like an unwritten rule; break it and it would be a crime.

Alfred stumbled up out of the bed to remove the pencil from the clock. He trudged over to the clock and carefully removed the splintered pencil. For a second, he thought he broke the gears, but it turned out it was a splinter (He found out by getting it stabbed inside of his finger, a painful account on his behalf). It was a successful mission in his eyes, with one casualty; a Ticonderoga pencil had been crushed by an insane amount of force. Alfred let out a sigh and cast the pencil into the trash.

Alfred then approached the kitchen to get his daily breakfast of bitter coffee, the only thing that helped him through the day. He struck a match and lit the kerosene stove. He poured a pint (a pint exact) of water into a pot which he set over the stove. It boiled as he poured two packets of powdered coffee into it (He had set them out the night before). He then yanked powdered creamer (There were a plentitude of powdered foods and liquids in the cabin) out of a little nook he called his "Storing nook."

He began to hum a blues tune as he sprinkled the powdered cream into the heating coffee. Alfred stirred the creamer into a white swirl. It reminded him of the Milky-Way galaxy, but instead of in space it was a cup of coffee. He chuckled at his brush with imagination (He hadn't come across the pal since his childhood). Then he poured the coffee into a homemade cup that said," #1 son!" This wasn't necessarily true, but Alfred kept the mug anyway.

(As soon as Alfred had graduated from college he moved far away from his family. A cabin retreat seemed nice and wonderful when Alfred had the idea, but it turned out to be a nightmare. The Ficklewood forest was certainly dense and far away from civilization, but Alfred didn't care. His new car was a

Mercedes-Benz Gullwing [Alfred is seventy-five years old, approaching seventy-six] and it seemed he could fly to the moon with it. Until it broke down.

He trudged along towards the nearest store with a thin rain slicker [It had been pouring outside, causing little marks on the paint of Alfred's house. The Dollar Tree rain slicker didn't hold up well in what would later be considered Ficklewood's worst storm]. Branches tore at the rain slicker whilst swaying in the harsh breeze. It was a nightmare walking through the muddy murk of the storm.

Then Alfred saw it. The neon sign with flashing LED lights seemed to light up the entire forest as he stared. The cacophony and craziness were blurred out by the amazing miracle. It was a miracle that Alfred made it, and so began his isolation. He never travelled and visited the gas station once a month to pick up supplies).

Alfred let out a sigh as he looked out of the window, watching deer frolic and birds singing. It was a nice and tranquil day, the bees buzzing and the butterflies flying. The Ficklewood forest stretched on for acres more, with many small beauties throughout. Nature wasn't always perfect, though. Occasionally, on one of these types of mornings, a predator would chase a deer, a rodent would gobble up a butterfly, or hopefully a squirrel would fall out of a tree.

Coffee was a favorite treat for Alfred when he watched the animals. His house had no running water (He used a pump and outhouse) or electricity, so this was his pastime. Watching nature.

The tick of the clock cast an eerie environment upon the peaceful scene. Deer looked more sinister, as if the brown splash of color around their eyes were shadows covering their face and the dots all over them were scars. Bee's stingers were razor sharp knives that could stab you right through your heart. Butterflies were bloodthirsty monsters that acted cute to intimidate you.

You may think that being in this situation you would be absolutely scared with a sight so terrifying. Alfred wasn't.

He was a strange man, that Alfred. If a bee ever stung a deer, he would smile. A butterfly eaten by a robin, a grin. If a bee's hive was knocked down by an animal (Mainly bears and occasionally a wolverine) the same smile crept on Alfred's face. His cruelty spread to humans, too. Once in high school he watched a boy carry pounds upon pounds of books into the school. Back then he was a bully, the one that wasn't invited to parties, asked to go on a date with, or even later to be invited to weddings (Even his friends began to consider him schizophrenic, and said he went "Around the bend" as an inside joke).

As I was saying, this boy walked by. He was a rather nerdy boy who was frequently called four eyes and super nerd (Childish insults. Even high schoolers were immature in name calling). He had five books (*World history, The History of the Americas, Africa's History, A Collection of European History, and Asia's History*) stacked in his hands. The boy was clearly struggling with a red face and shaky muscles. He veered from side to side, attempting to avoid his fellow schoolmates.

As the boy got farther down the hall, Alfred had a devious idea. Alfred took a large step in front of the boy. They were next to locker 478, the boy's locker. He reached his hand over to unlock his lock, but Alfred grabbed it. He glared at the boy and slapped the books out of his hands. Alfred chuckled as the boy scrambled to pick his books up. Alfred's friend, Jack, looked at him in disgust. Jack, too, was a bit of a bully in the name calling game.

Alfred looked back at himself in that situation, seeing his best friend glare at him so sinisterly, as if Alfred was a monster. That look of distrust and disgust for his average game haunted Alfred.

Back to the story. Alfred stared intently at the theater that was "Nature." It was the bee attacking a racoon that reminded Alfred to reload the gun.

Ever since he could remember, Alfred kept a bolt action rifle by his doorway. The gun's barrel always remained loaded. It's sleek design and barrel could scare the bravest man in the room out of his wits. That gun had shot before (On accident) and blood poured out of the victim. It was a deer he had killed, and he felt so guilty he never did it again.

A thought surfaced in his head; *Did I load that rifle?* He had a packet of 5.56 caliber ammo locked deep inside of a closet. It was well hidden inside a shoebox, with a jacket covering that shoebox.

Alfred rose from his comfortable, leather couch (It had several tears, but it remained a beautiful bit of furniture to him). He waltzed over to the closet. Then he shook the closet doorknob. It wouldn't budge so he kicked it open. Inside were old leather jackets and blazers that were out of style.

Alfred crouched down beside the blazer (It had a vicious tiger leaping toward an unsuspecting caribou. It was entirely unrealistic, but it was his "Best in collection." It wasn't very nice, though, considering blood. The tiger's teeth were stained with blood, another previous victim. The caribou also had a cut). With a sweep of the hand he moved the blazer. Underneath was a shoebox with the words," Ammo 5.56" written on it (It was a blue sharpie, which was partially dried out. That's why the words on the box were faded. Not from time. The sharpie was guilty for it). He lifted the two flaps and fished around for the packet of ammo. His hand wrapped around a cold, metal 5.56 caliber bullet.

Alfred trotted over to the gun with some bullets in his hand. It was a rather mundane march between point A and B. He had bland taste, with the wallpaper a melancholy white. Ceiling, walls, and even the floor were white. A shade of grey was used for bedrooms, whilst brown was used for the kitchen.

Alfred inspected the gun and found it was loaded when he shot the gun on accident (He shot it right through the door. Right. Through. The. Door.). *Damn it* he thought. *Damn, damn, damn!*

The gun was lifted, reloaded, and set back down. An angry Alfred stomped back to his couch and kicked a chair. His rage boiled up inside as he sat. If he hadn't sat down and taken deep breaths, his emotions might've blown into an ugly rainbow of rage.

Alfred sat down onto the couch (If anything it was a bench with a leathery skin) with a large thud. The thud echoed around inside of the hollow couch. He went back to drinking his coffee, but now it was very cold. Alfred's face cringed in disgust from the coffee's bitter taste. He took another sip and returned to his joyous watching of nature.

A storm began to brew at the hour of thirteen. Dark clouds swirled into a mix as they prepared to release rain upon the world. The deer, bees, and butterflies retreated knowing that they were going to be stormed upon. Alfred listened to the peaceful rat-a-tap-tapping of the rain. It banged against the house's white paint job, rubbing some off. Alfred didn't mind, for surely no one would see it.

Benny Jackson approached the rain beaten house a few feet in front of him. His car lights flashed over and over on the petite house. They seemed to purposely cast a creepy glow, warning him to stay away. *After all, it's not like some psycho lived here. Not like Casper lives here, either! It's just an old abandoned house* Benny reassured himself. The house beckoned him but also warned him; it sent mixed messages right toward him, playing a tug-of-war game that would last forever.

His leg had a deep gash from his knee down. Fresh blood ran down his skinny leg to his white socks. He was almost certain that he had broken his left leg and left elbow. Both were non-moveable, so Benny was left crawling toward the dimly lit house. The slick ground soaked him through his dollar tree bought rain slicker. Dirt stained his white Fraggle Rock t-shirt.

Have to get inside before the flooding begins he repeatedly reminded himself. That was the only reason he pushed on. Any other time and he would be lying there with two fractures and slowly bleeding to death, taking short, shallow breaths. By the next hour he would've died from lack of oxygen.

"Please," Ben cried out into the darkness of the night. It wasn't like he knew anybody was there, so I am still clueless to why Benny kept calling.

"Please, help..."

With his remaining strength he scaled the stairs leading up to the porch, each old and worn. They were even more slippery than the ground, and Benny almost slipped a couple times, but he pushed up and up till the top. Blood poured down the steps as he finished up the treacherous climb.

Benny noticed a small hole in the door, with a bullet resting about an inch in front of it. Adrenaline (*Damn it adrenaline! At Six Flags you go off right away but now in my one deadly situation you're late?*) rushed through his almost lifeless body. He grabbed for the door-handle and pulled (With his right arm, of course). As soon as the door opened, he was greeted with the butt of a rifle to his head.

"Screw it! This arm needs to be amputated!" Alfred exclaimed as he bandaged up Benny. Benny was unconscious with two fractures and a deadly gash that were covered in either plaster or gauze (Alfred had studied to be a professional doctor. He had old medical supplies). Alfred had saved Benny in the matter of an hour.

An exhausted Benny woke up from his slumber to find a drizzle of blood (It was from when Alfred hit him with the gun) on his forehead and plaster wrapped around his left arm and leg. He was lying on a firm mattress in the middle of Alfred's living room. It was strange to Benny that there were no pictures or art pieces in the entire room. The only things in the room were a couch (He thought it was a bench covered in leather) and grandfather clock. He could see their reflection (Barely) in the rusty pendulum of the clock. It swung to and fro, changing images from the bench to them.

"Wakey wakey," Alfred told him.

"Who are you?" Ben asked with dread.

"Who are you?" Alfred asked with a sudden brusqueness in his voice.

"Car crash. Storm started. And by the way, my name is Benny. NOT Ben."

"Ah. Well I'm Alfred. You may have read one of my stories in the paper."

He made a gesture towards an old, rusty typewriter (It seemed everything in this house had rust in some form on it). Its keys seemed worn with fading labels. The paint seemed to have worn off some.

"Tell me *Benny*, where do you work?"

"GCal. I'm stuck in QA, looking over the decals we make. 'Well I found that this T is not at a 30-degree angle!' and 'You misspelled this' are literally the only things my colleagues say. I, though, stay in the cafeteria by pretending I spilt ketchup all over myself on accident. Then I reside in a bathroom stall until two o' clock. I examine the decals and pick the cool ones. Once I smuggled a few cool decals home with me."

"That seems like an... interesting job."

Alfred made sure to not ask that question ever again. After all, he was practically told Benny's life story!

"I just publish articles. Published a few essays and short stories, too. So how did this happen, exactly?" Alfred asked.

"All I have to say, Mr. Alfred, is that I got a work trip. Was visiting the town of Clinton. GCal headquarters is in Clinton. *Was* going to meet the boss. Storm starts. Car crash. I was in debt. Only had a rain slicker from the Dollar Tree."

Benny realized that he was still wearing that rain slicker. It was covered in dirt and blood, and most noticeable, tears. It was entirely shredded, with little scraps that had come off.

Alfred related to Benny with being in debt. His Gullwing was bought from a loan and he couldn't repay it. He turned to news writing later, and payed the Gullwing off (Including penalty fees) the year before. *If I hadn't bought the Gullwing* Alfred thought *I could've possibly avoided the crash. I might've had enough to buy a decent rain slicker.*

"Well that sounds interesting Mr. Benny. May I ask you a question?

"Sure."

"How do you not feel pain? I mean, it was only an hour ago you arrived."

Benny pondered this. He would openly admit he didn't know how. His life was full of pain. As a teenager he got injuries constantly. A cut here, a broken bone there. Once he got a gash across his arm, through his chest, and to his other arm. It was brutal that day, but Benny just got back up and skated around. He then passed out from blood loss, but that's beside the point.

"Guess I just have a knack," Benny smiled. It was true he had a "knack." Once at three years he broke his toe. He simply shed a tear and told his mom, even though she could tell (It was flipped to the side, stuck that way).

Alfred rolled his eyes as Benny's head fell to the mattress.

"No please no!" Benny muttered under his breath as he lay in a slumber. He couldn't make out what was in the corner, but he knew it wasn't good.

"Now that the storm has come, I have!" a raspy voice exclaimed

"Comingggggg..."

The shadows engulfed him in an envelope of darkness. All he could see was darkness plastered against the dimly lit room as if a canvas.

Then it turned to a peaceful neighborhood. His neighborhood.

There was a slight breeze that encouraged his American Flag to do a jig (He was very patriotic with

American flag t-shirts and trinkets). Leaves were lying in the roads, with many a color. There was a nice rustle in the bushes. But there wasn't an animal in the bushes. It was a bloodthirsty monster.

It had razor-sharp teeth and hideous green fur. Its nose was turned upward, and its chin pushed in. Its eyes were deep inside its skull, staring intently into its victim's soul. Its ears pointed up and curved like a bat's. Its claws were like a human's but stuck farther out and were sharp. Its toenails curved inward instead of out. It stood at a whopping 9 foot 6.

The beast pushed down the trees in Benny's front yard. It took out sticks and threw them towards Benny. He let out a cry of pure terror. The monster seemed to flinch, perhaps from its large ears.

"Comingggggg..." echoed through Benny's head again as he was whisked down the street. Against his free will Benny waddled down the street. He saw the old McDonald family's house (Truly it was an elderly couple's house, Mr. and Mrs. McDonald's. They were around the age of eighty) and Brown family's house. They were lit up by street lights that towered over Benny. There were no signs of activity inside the houses. They seemed untouched and looked beautiful (To be honest, though, it was always like that. The families stayed inside from constant rain storms.

Benny didn't have time to take in the scenery. He was involuntarily sliding across the concrete sidewalk.

"I'm sorry, I would like to go home, so-," Benny began to ask rhetorically. The monster let out a hiss that seemed to come right from deep inside him. It was more of a roar that was toned down a level.

At the end of the cul-de-sac was a girl. Black hair draped over her shoulders. She wore a pink dress and had a red bow in her hair. A balloon was tied around the girl's wrist.

The girl began to mess with the balloon string. It was tightened with great force, so the girl was struggling.

After a painful moment the balloon took off. It flew up, up, up. The monster put his hand on the girl's shoulder, and a despicable smile spread across its face.

"Comingggggggggggg!"

Benny sat up with a sudden jolt of energy. He took shallow breaths and looked up at the clock. The time was 4:59. A whole minute since he fell asleep.

Sweat rolled down Benny's head, and his cut felt worse from the sodium in his sweat.

"What's wrong? Did wittle Benny have a nightmare?" Alfred teased. Benny couldn't do anything. He just fell back onto his cot in shock. His face smooshed up in disgust and fear. *What the HELL was that?* Benny thought.

Benny's right arm twitched around a bit, along with the fingers on his left arm. His eyes squinted into little slits at the horror he had just witnessed.

"Gu gu gu guuu..." he stuttered. Benny's eyes opened wide from the slits, so he looked like a three-year-old staring through a Hamleys window.

"Are you okay Benny?" Alfred asked with a sudden curiosity. He crossed his fingers inside of his pockets and began to sweat. Benny truly looked in shock. *He's scaring the living daylights out me* Alfred thought with a sense of dread. Alfred himself wanted to tremble like a little baby, but he decided against it.

"Seriously, are you okay?"

"Comingggggggggggg," was all Benny mustered out before falling back onto the linen pillow (It had roses entwined on the front and doves pulling the roses in an endless tug-of-war. It was a better display of love than Alfred's wretched blazer).

Alfred took a deep breath and counted to ten. Benny turned white as snow and looked as if he were a ghost freshly reanimated. His eyes seemed to roll back in their sockets, as if Benny was dying. A shocked Alfred's jaw dropped as he watched such an oddity, for the spectacle was unbeknownst to Alfred until that day. He thought that Benny may be faking, but he was still cautious.

Alfred found that he should lay down a bit. The day's festivities were too much. Deep down inside Alfred's gut he could tell that there would be a horrific uprising of truly terrible events.

He waddled over to his bed (He was a bowl-legged man) and poured some Alka-Seltzer into a glass of water. It popped and fizzed inside of its glass prison. Gravity pulled the Alka-Seltzer deeper and deeper into the abyss until it was fully dissolved.

Alfred grabbed the glass and gulped down the medicinal water. It relieved him of his stomach's uneasiness right away, a job well done. A sigh of relief managed to slip out of Alfred. But even though he felt a little better, tensions weren't entirely eradicated. He still had an urge

To Murder

to make Benny leave.

After all he had been through (Benny, nature, treatment, and fear) he felt better. No longer did Alfred have

To Murder

to think such violent thoughts.

He lay down

To Murder

to go to sleep. He picked up one of his all-time favorite novels, *Misery*, and began to read.

"Writers remember everything... especially the hurts. Strip a writer to the buff, point to the scars, and he'll tell you the story of each small one. From the big ones you get novels. A little talent is a nice thing to have if you want to be a writer, but the only real requirement is the ability to remember the story of every scar. Art consists of the persistence of memory," was all he managed to read before he heard it.

It slammed against the roof with the might of a thousand men, it let the water leak in, and it screeched," Comingggggggggggg!" from the outside.

That was the only noise Alfred heard that night other than the dripping water and midnight chime. The only thing. Water. Not a scream. Not a slap. Not a punch. Not a snore. Only water.

But there is one noise I forgot to mention. The clock. The clock's tick blended in with the dripping of the water. It ticked when the water dripped. It sang when the water sang. It stopped when the water stopped. They performed in an almost perfect chorus, their two unique sounds blending. The clock was the quiet one, the water the loud.

With every drip and every tick came the same two words inside Alfred; To Murder. *To Murder, stop, To Murder, mind, To Murder, telling, To Murder, me, To Murder, this!* was all Alfred could get out in his mind. He fought his insanity (He had had an evil side all his life, a true evil side. It wasn't petty things like "Eat three Oreos instead of two," but eviler like "Punch him." That's why Alfred had so much trouble with anger management).

To Murder.

Alfred lay his head on the pillow and grabbed his ear-defenders (Sometimes in the morning birds would chirp, so he wore the ear-defenders to sleep in). He slid them over his left, then right, ears.

The silence greeted Alfred like an old friend. It drowned out the world and cut him off from reality. He was in a peaceful place where he could think clear thoughts without constant distractions.

Benny's out to murder me Alfred thought. *Benny wants me dead. He probably snuck outside, climbed on the roof, and banged the house in. He wants me distracted so he puts on a little show. He purposely crashed that car. He knew the storm was coming. He wants me dead!*

Alfred, after a long period of pondering, fell asleep. Drool fell from his mouth. The pain of his achy bones was not felt. His mind brewed him up a nightmare unwillingly. He watched. And he watched. And watched. He watched Benny sharpen an axe in his dream. The hatchet glimmered in an extraterrestrial light cast from the stained glass at the top of his house (The only window). Benny raised it and slashed around, his face straining from using his force to sling the axe around. His eyes glimmered with red light, giving him an unearthly appearance. Slowly but surely his ears curled up, his eyes went farther and farther inside his head, his green clothes turned into fur, his nose turned up like a pig's, and he grew an extra three feet.

"Comingggggggggggg," Benny hissed. With a final burst of energy, he slashed the axe. It would have hit Alfred directly if not for the setting change. From his living room came the woods on a nice sunny day. Sunlight sifted through the mighty tree branches jutting out from the beautiful oak trees. Then Alfred saw himself running.

The Alfred in the dream was panting, moving around a meter every five seconds. Sweat rolled down

(His? Their?) the Alfred's wrinkled face. Benny threw that axe through the air, and real Alfred saw himself die. The triumphant Benny let out a roar of pride. He stood on the Alfred's lifeless body.

Alfred awoke to hear the clock go off. It struck the hour of midnight, and the second day began.

The SECOND Day

Alfred sat upright in bed as the clock chimed the hour of (24 or 1?) midnight. He stared intently at Benny, who looked like a ragdoll strewn about, and thought.

To Murder

Who is this man? Does he truly work for GCal or is he a liar? echoed around his head. It was pinging around like a pinball, scoring ten-thousand points total.

After a long five minutes of contemplating, Alfred got up. He grabbed Benny's small

To Murder

sack and rummaged through it. He found nothing deadly looking, so Alfred gave up.

He returned to his bed. With a last reassuring glance toward Benny, Alfred lay down. He closed his eyes and sighed.

Almost instantly he fell into a deep slumber.

Benny woke up at the stroke of ten. Chiming echoed through his mind as he got up (He was very dizzy). He stumbled to the side as the world turned sideways, and he had to steady himself multiple times. Alfred hung halfway off of the bed, so he pondered fixing his position. Benny decided against it, for he might wake his new innkeeper up. He wanted to remain the tenant.

Now how do things work in the mornings? Benny wondered. He had never stayed inside such a place, one without electricity.

To Murder

What?

To Murder

A sudden wave of fear flooded into Benny's body. His leg twitched.

After a minute he realized he was dreaming. He looked down at his legs. Functional.

But he couldn't have been dreaming. No, it was all too real. Benny tried to fly, but he couldn't. *Not dreaming.*

To Murder

It was as if Benny had a magical spell cast on him that granted the "Victim" invincibility (Or at least some invincibility). He looked down at his elbow. It, too, was okay. The gash was missing, and his sock was strangely ridden of blood. Not even the tiniest scar was on his body.

What the HELL is wrong with me?

To Murder

Benny was on the brink of a freak-out. He had the sudden

To Murder

urge to look in a mirror. Ever since he could remember he had a scar above his eyebrow. As a child his head had hit the corner of a table. It had bled, and bled, and bled. Benny was lucky to have survived.

Benny dashed over to the kitchen, where the closest mirror was. The scar was gone. Instead there was a small crease on his skin where the scar had been.

To Murder

"Oh my-" Benny stuttered. He let out a shriek that was powerful enough to cause Alfred to stir.

What the hell is happening? Alfred

To Murder

asked in his mind. Adrenaline pumped through his old veins as he got up. *What is Benny doing this-*

Then Alfred heard it. The clock.

He rounded the doorway and glanced at the time piece. It showed that it was 10:25. *Got to wind in the weight.*

31

To Murder

"What's wrong you weirdo!" Alfred asked with a sudden tumultuous tone.

"My bones- my scar- my leg-," Benny stuttered in a confused fashion. His muscles went limp and he squatted a tiny bit.

"Spit it out!"

"B-B-But w-what? H-how?"

A wave of trepidation swept across Alfred. Like Benny he began to stutter.

"W-what do y-you m-m-mean?"

Benny was able to finally say what he wanted to with clarity.

"My wounds are healed."

Alfred noticed that he was okay, in health standards at least. His broken bones and fractures were fully fixed. *Saves me the trouble of amputating that damn thing.*

To Murder Alfred

Benny's mind whisked up that thought. From deep, deep inside his subconscious it began. It slowly seeped through the barrier that was good and invaded his entire mind. His body's gears ran on the grinding letters of *To Murder Alfred* for the night. The powder fell into a pile, then to a hill, then to a mountain. A piece of splintered-off evil stabbed his thought-process and corrupted everything in its path. His good intentions were defeated in a popularity contest that was rigged.

"Mr. Alfred, I'm sca-scared," Benny whispered under his breath. The stutter was back.

"Don't worry," Alfred reassured Benny, but he was mainly trying to feel better about everything himself. *This is the weirdest day of my life. Can I fly?* Alfred thought. He attempted to spread his angelic wings and fly to the stars, but instead he was greeted by a tumble that could have been deadly for his age. His wrinkly, achy legs pressed up against his butt as he jumped. Alfred wrapped his hands around his knobby knees to make sure his thighs didn't touch the floor again.

With an echoing *thud* Alfred collided with the ground. His head banged hard against the wooden floor. A small snapping noise came from his neck, but he was seemingly fine. All dignity inside of Alfred left in a swift exhale of breath. Pain shot from his legs then out of his body, a truly electrifying experience. His eyes opened wide and he saw a flash of red.

"Are you- s-sane a-anymore?" Benny asked inquisitively. His face cringed in disgust at the horrific sight of some bozo recluse who lives in the Ficklewood forest (What an appropriate name for a horror story) that just happens to be insane and leaping into the air to purposely injure himself.

"Sorry. Just checking if I'm dreaming. Now, what the hell is happening?" Alfred asked in what a much calmer voice was. After all, the impossible just happened and nobody knew why (Well, isn't everything impossible unexplainable?). Something horrific was beginning to unfurl. Something that even the daftest of people could see (The British in me) is beginning to slowly stalk them into a corner. Something bad. No, there is no mere way to truly express this in word form. "Terrible" is not enough. Not even the word cataclysmic can describe the process of this tale.

"I don't know, Mr. Alfred. I truly don't know."

Benny sat next to Alfred on the bench. He twiddled his thumbs and blew on his hands to prevent overheating from the clammy air. It was humid inside of the cabin, with a nice mixture of moisture in the air. Bad vibes (Long-hair surfer dude part of me) radiated off both the grown men, their faces looking solemn and confused. Both of their hair looked frizzled and unkept; it was all over the place, tied in knots or on the wrong side of the part. Both were also unshaven and little specks of hair surrounded their mouths. "Whiskers" both called them.

Silence clouded around the two, keeping their lips stuck closed. Alfred wore his tiger-caribou-murder-scene blazer, some torn jeans, and a stained white shirt under the blazer. Benny wore some trousers, a white shirt, and a torn rain slicker (Alfred's this time).

"Want some coffee?" Alfred asked, breaking the silence that seemed to go on for centuries.

Benny replied in a quieter voice," Yes please, Mr. Alfred."

Alfred took a moment to marvel at Benny's manners. The teens at the gas station just shoved your goods in a bag and threw them at you. They all just wanted to go to the McDonald's across the street to hang out with their friends and do some graffiti. They would throw rocks at passing cars if they could find any (Alfred remembered them throwing rocks at his automobile and him giving them an unpleasant finger in return). Then they would get on their social medias and post about how they "cracked the principal's windshield." If Clinton had a police force (Which they don't) all those damn teens would be long gone, but since Clinton was so small, they relied on a town twenty miles away.

Alfred lumbered into the kitchen and grabbed eight packets of joe out of the storing nook.

"Hey Benny! Can you go outside and get some water from the pump?"

"Sure Mr. Alfred! I'll happily oblige!"

Benny walked without even the slightest limp. He felt like a three-year-old boy again, running gleefully through tall, slender grass fields. So, with the energy of a thousand five-year-old kids, Benny walked outside. The smell of nature filled his nostrils and stayed there. All the good smelling things including pines, honeysuckle, and more mixed together to make a wonderous concoction. Benny's mind filled with nice things, as if all the bad things had escaped and were fleeing punishments.

To Murder

Benny didn't pay attention to that that time. Instead he skipped across the grassy turf that covered the rocks surrounding Alfred's house (Rocks were buried around 10 feet under the Ficklewood forest. It had been a popular quarry zone). The red pump rested around the back of the house, looking ready to crank out water. Its handle jutted out from the top of the works. Rust gave it a fine coat, and made it look older than it truly was. It was like the reverse of those anti-age creams.

Benny grasped an old iron bucket resting next to the pump and placed it under the pipe. He then grabbed the handle and held on firmly. With all his might Benny was able to get water to pour out of the small pump by cranking the damn pump up and down in a repeated fashion. Water sloshed around in the metal bucket, making a mini tsunami.

After about a minute Benny stopped the water, and thirty seconds after that the water was still and placid inside the dented canister. It went back to its swaying ways when Benny carried the cask inside of the shed. As Benny circumnavigated around the corner by the door and kitchen, Alfred grew a tiny bit less impatient. With a loud thud, the bucket collided with the surface of the counter.

"Thank you, Benny. You're a lifesaver!"

Benny sat back down whilst Alfred turned on the kerosene stove.

"Hey Benny? Can you wind up the weight in that clock over there?"

"Eh, sure Mr. Alfred!"

Benny searched for a key on top of the grandfather clock. After a long and rigorous moment of searching, the key was found. It was thin and had a decorated handle (A bee was inside a diamond). The smell of smoke drifted into the living room. A steady tick answered in return as Benny slid the key into its slot. He twisted it and pulled the door open. Inside rested the pendulum, several gears, and a string tied around a lead weight. The other end of the string was strewn over a wooden box at the top. With a small amount of force Benny pulled the string, and the weight went up next to the box. He slammed the doors close and locked both. Next, he walked next to the island.

In the kitchen (On the island) were two steaming cups of creamed coffee. Both had white swirls inside that had been stirred into little triangles and squares. One was darker than the other, perhaps because more packets were poured in that specific one.

Benny grabbed the coffee with more caffeine. He took a sip and ran to the couch. With a thud he sat down. It echoed around inside of the hut.

To Murder Alfred

There it was again! Benny's mind had stooped low again. No longer would it think that again after a nice, long drink of a cup of Joe.

Alfred sat down next to Benny. Both stared through the large stained-glass window at a distorted view of nature. Both took a sip and were instantly in heaven.

Nothing had happened.

This is a whole four hours since we last caught up with our characters (I refuse to call them heroes!). At three o' clock (Now in the story) they cracked out a few cases of beer and two bottles of whiskey. Benny grabbed a Bud light and drank up. Alfred grabbed a bottle of whiskey and finished it within the hour.

"So, Alfred, tell me the worst time in your life," Benny asked in a slurred voice. It was no surprise since this was his second bottle of beer in ten minutes.

"Eh, I was an alcoholic. Had a wife. Left this dump for a bit. Luckily while I was away nobody bid on the house. Anyhow, out of here. Just sitten' in a chair across from 'er. She was beautiful. Back to story. Got drunk on a few cans. Got mad. Sued for being abusive by hitting her across the face. Spent a whole damn year in a prison. I was bailed out. Those men are assholes up in Clinton. Long story short my wife married again, had a couple kids. I'm left alone in the dumps, vowing to never drink again. But here you come, and boy am I glad you did. Excuses to drink!" Alfred explained with a chuckle here or there. A few hours previous they had been discussing alcohol. When Alfred thought the time right, he whipped out the cases which lay on the floor.

"Time I regret most is debt. Got a girlfriend. Had a lot money. Wasted it. Owed money. Now here I am working for GCal for ten cents a minute. GCal is run by assholes! Every day is a budget cut. First the water machine, then the coffee, and finally six dollars shaved off ever worker's salary, except for the damn managers and higher positions!" Benny cried in a frenzy of rage. His eyes had little flames burning inside, refusing to bow down to superiors.

"GCal sounds like crap. I can do ya' one better. Tures industries. Just when they started was terrible. That was when I was actually married!" Alfred joined Benny's ailments.

"Ah, GCal's a way of life. After a bit of working with a few corporate assholes you get used to it."

Benny picked his third beer up from the floor and popped the beer-cap. It fell with a clunk on the hard wood floors. He took another sip and belched.

"Now I'm going to quit. Maybe I become a substitute teacher and teach them kiddos."

Benny got up from his position and walked to the mattress (It was still there, even after the day previous).

"Good night, fellow idiot. See you tomorrow."

To Murder

Alfred got up at the stroke of 19. For the second time he had forgotten to stop the clock. *Damn it.*

Something surfaced in Alfred's mind. Something horrible. Something that brought him to insanity,

Get out of this damn bed. Go get the gun. Wait for Benny to wake up and- oh crap, I have one hell of a hangover! Ohhh-

Alfred's head hurt. It was the worst headache he had ever had in his entire life. His nose was also running, and he thought he had the flu (Or a cold). Then Alfred got up. He walked to the door and grabbed the sleek weapon.

Benny woke up with a hangover. He was sick, his head hurt, and he felt very weak. At times he twitched in his sleep, other times he coughed.

"Hey Mr. Alfred? You got a hangover t-" Benny managed to say before the bang happened.

Alfred had pulled the trigger. His loaded gun spit out a couple bullets in Benny's direction. Both hit him within a second. He let out a low moan before dying.

Alfred let out a chuckle. No, let's be real. He let out a maniacal laughter that could cripple any old beautiful thing. *Noooo-* was all the old Alfred could think. Now he was new. Not nicer. Meaner. More brutal.

No longer was there an Alfred. All there was was a murderer.

Alfred dragged Benny outside into the cool night air. His lifeless ragdoll body was clad in only a Fraggle Rock shirt and underwear. Both began to stain from the dirt.

Benny seemed to stare deep inside of Alfred's soul. His eyesight burned a hole through Alfred's skin and out of his body. He didn't care and just kept dragging.

In Alfred's left hand was a shovel. It had a sharp, metal tip that could obviously dig well. The metal was stained with dirt from previous digging expeditions.

"Hello, Benny, old friend. You're six. Feet. Under," Alfred taunted. He began digging a hole. After a few minutes, he kicked the body into the hole. It rolled around on the steep sides of the hole. Almost immediately Alfred began to fill the hole back up.

At the end of the mission he gave the earth a reassuring pat. Alfred chuckled (He was still drunk). It started as nothing much but escalated into something

else. A demoniac laugh, a monstrous laugh. And Alfred
left it at that.

Alfred heard it. A rustle.

Something had brushed against a bush outside.
Something big.

He went outside to check on everything.

At first he treated it as a joke.

He banged against his chest and made gorilla
noises.

Then it happened.

He saw it.

It saw him.

He ran.

It chased.

He tripped.

It ate.

The Press

Recently a famous author has been killed. Mr. Alfred Lee, one of our publishers, has sadly perished. It is believed a wild bear has mauled him after his autopsy. In other news, GCal worker Benny Jackson is still missing. If any news is found about him, please report to 911.

Epilogue

Victoria Small walked through the antique store that was on the corner of GCal and McDonalds with her son, Marcus. She had heard in the paper that there was sale on some antiques they had found in some writer named Alfred's house, and sure enough, a piece of paper with the words *20% off! What a steal!* printed on it was attached to a majority of the antiques in the *NEW!* section.

Damn it, why did mom have to drag me

to this crappy joint in the middle of rush hour

when I could be sitting on the couch with Bill

instead?

Silver vases and pendulums turned into "modern art" resided amongst the window display that had once drawn Victoria into the small, run down stand-alone building, but the art had truly sold it. The antique store was known all the way to Middingstone for its noticeable art collection that had such bright hues that it made the melancholy room seem comfortable. Marcus thought the paintings stared at him when he walked past.

Victoria marveled at a clock that stood out among the remaining antiques. It was beautiful and must have been old (She could tell from some wood eaten by termites). The grandfather clock remained on even though it had a beaten state, caused by the rough drive from the old man's house to the store.

"Its beautiful! Perfect! I must have it!" Victoria exclaimed. Her eyes lit up in a flame of delight that refused to be fanned. The wallet that previously sheltered inside of her pocket was removed, and lifted up, up into the air.

Marcus crouched down to eye level with the silver pendulum. It reflected him until it didn't.

For what may have been one, maybe two swings, he didn't see himself. It was something... different. He was green and had a pig-like nose, along with bat ears that seemed to home in on every little sound.

Marcus was scared – very scared – of the clock.

"I'll take it!" Victoria cried as she handed the cashier her well earned money. They rang it up on their bit of machinery that seemed impossible to understand with all it's different slots.

And, with a creepy touch to it, the clock rang. Then the thing that put Marcus unconscious occurred, the thing that was never mentioned again in the Smalls household. The words "To Murder."

Special thanks to...

- Both of my parents, who read my story
  during the process of "writing."

- All of my grandparents, who I knew would root for me if they knew I was writing
- My teacher, who pushed us all to write in class
- Stephen King's *The Shining*, which inspired me to write this
- Steve DeGroof, who wrote an *Instructables* page about *LuLu*, my publishing service
- LuLu, for their eBook and printing options

About the Author

Kingsley Dockerill is an 11-year-old author who is obsessed with all horror. His family is highly encouraging and have always supported his crazy dreams.